NAKED TWISTER

AN EROTIC ADVENTURE

VICTORIA RUSH

VOLUME 37

JADE'S EROTIC ADVENTURES - BOOK 37

COPYRIGHT

For the uninhibited...

WANT TO AMP UP YOUR SEX LIFE?

Sign up for my newsletter to receive more free books and other steamy stuff. Discover a hundred different ways to wet your whistle!

Victoria Rush Erotica

1

____

When I saw the new email message from my friend Madison with the cryptic heading *Don't get your knickers in a knot*, I had to open it right away. Madison was famous for hosting the most interesting and sexy parties, and as I began to read the message, I could already feel my heart racing in excitement.

Dear Jade,

You are cordially invited to a party at Madison's place this Saturday at 9 p.m.

As with my other events, there will be a special activity that will be sure to keep everyone engaged and spread the love around. I don't want to spoil the surprise by giving away too much, other than asking you to wear loose fitting or stretchy clothing.

And you might also want to work on strengthening your abs at the gym or the yoga studio. Because you're going to need a fair amount of 'stamina' to play the game I have in mind.

I think you'll find this variation on a classic game will be sure to please! Be there or be square,

Maddy

P.S.: Make sure you're freshly polished and scrubbed, and I do mean everywhere, because you know, one thing often leads to another at my parties. ;-)

What the–? I thought, as my mind raced trying to decipher what she was cooking up this time. *It's going to be some kind of 'physical' game requiring strength and stamina, and it sounds like there's going to be a fair amount of body contact, with or without clothes. It could be anything from flag football to dodgeball to nerf tag.*

After stewing over what she had planned for most of the day, I finally succumbed later that evening and gave her a ring.

"Hey, sexy!" she answered, after seeing my caller ID on her phone.

"You know I can't sit on that mysterious invitation without wanting to pry for more details."

"Pry away," she teased. "But you're not going to get much more out of me. Finding out what the surprise is when you get here is half the fun. Plus, I want everybody to be charged up and ready to jump in the moment they arrive."

"Jump in?" I said. "Does it involve your swimming pool?"

"At some point it's pretty likely," she said. "If only to cool off after all the strenuous exercise. And I'm pretty sure most of the attendees will have their clothes stripped off within an hour or so, so it seems like a logical place to finish off."

"You are *such* a tease!" I huffed, more confused than ever about what she had planned. "Who's invited?"

"It's a pretty mixed bag," she said, knowing my preference for sex with women. "Some people you know, plus a few new faces. But I can guarantee they're all hot! You might even be tempted to switch sides once or twice during all the merrymaking."

"Jesus, Mad!" I squealed into the phone. "You're killing me!"

"That's the whole idea," she said. "I want you to be on pins and needles by the time you arrive at the party. And to keep your options open. Because there's going to be a fair amount of random touching and interaction. Who *knows* what body parts might get intermingled others during all the hijinks?"

"Where do you come up with these crazy ideas, anyway?" I said, marveling at her ingenuity in finding ever more creative and exciting games.

"What can I say?" she said. "I guess I'm just a kinky kind of girl."

"You got *that* right," I smiled, reflecting back on our last erotic encounter at her previous game night involving blindfolds. "But I can't guarantee I'm going to be all polished and pristine by the time I get there. I'm *already* getting wet imagining what you've got in store this time."

"Don't you worry your pretty little pussy over it," she said. "A little extra lubrication might come in handy in more ways than one for what I have in mind. And I use the word 'come' very loosely in this context."

"Fuck you," I said, playfully.

"Mmm, I hope so," she purred. "But it will depend which way the bottle spins..."

"Bottle?!" I said, shaking my head. "What does a bottle have to do–"

"See you Saturday at nine," she said. "And don't be late. This will be an all-hands-on-deck kind of activity. You don't want to miss your chance to get in on the action early."

When Madison hung up on me, I was tempted to call

her back, but I knew from previous experience that she wouldn't reveal any more details. Even though I was one of her closest confidants, she knew how quickly gossip traveled around our close-knit group of friends. And she also knew me well enough to know that the less knowledge I had about the details of her sexy party event, the more turned on and eager I'd be to play her game.

You got that right, girl, I smiled as I pulled my panties down and began to finger my soaking slit.

2

O n the night of Madison's party, I drove to her place with a certain degree of trepidation. The only loose clothing I could find in my closet were an old pair of flannel pajamas. I'd considered wearing my stretchy yoga tights, but with my tendency to soak my crotch when I got worked up, I figured the pajamas would help protect my modesty–at least until things heated up later in the evening. Besides, I still wasn't sold on the idea of touching my intimate body parts with a bunch of unknown men, and the thick material would provide an extra degree of insulation.

When I arrived at her house and she opened the door, she eyed my ensemble up and down, then smiled and nodded.

"A bit unconventional, but that'll do," she said. "Come on, we're just about ready to get started."

I could hear the buzz of male and female voices coming from her living room, and when she escorted me to the group, I was surprised to see a dozen or so people sitting barefoot around a plastic Twister mat on the floor.

Of course, I thought, shaking my head at my stupidity. *Stretching, exercise, random touching of body parts. How could I not have figured this one out?*

I peered around the group, recognizing a few of my friends. There was my BFF, Hannah, of course, plus a couple of girls from the office where Madison and I used to work. But there was also a fair number of unfamiliar faces of both genders. My pussy twitched as I scanned the group, noticing quite a few hot and sexy bodies bedecked in tight yoga outfits and skimpy gym clothes. And I smiled when I recognized my transgender friend Shae, who worked as a dancer at the local cabaret club. We'd shared an impassioned weekend together a few months ago, and I was suddenly glad I'd chosen the loose-fitting pajamas to wear as a dribble of lubrication trickled down the inside of my thigh.

"Now that we've got the last member of our group here," Madison said. "Let's finish up with the introductions. Most of you know Jade of course, but we also have a few new faces in the crowd.

"This is my friend Natalie from work," Maddy said, motioning to a cute blond girl in her twenties.

"And my college roommate, Taylor," who's in town for a few days visiting family.

"And my sexy neighbor Laura, who I'm totally envious of stealing all the attention on our block while she suntans all day long in her skimpy bikini around her pool."

I could see a number of both men and women around the circle nodding as they eyed her sylphlike body wrapped up in a tight two-piece yoga uniform.

"And on the other side of the mat," Maddy said, motioning to an equal number of men seated opposite the women. "Besides Dylan, Jake, and Marco, who you already know, we have my ex-boyfriend Brett, my current partner-in-crime Tyler, and Laura's husband Brad."

I glanced at each of the men and nodded, lingering for a little longer at Laura's husband, with his smoldering eyes and chiseled jaw. He was wearing a tight-fitting pair of sweat pants and a tank-top that showed off his perfectly sculpted athletic figure. Apparently I wasn't the only one distracted by his good looks and hot body, noticing some of the men frowning that his pretty wife Laura was already taken, while the women simply gawked at him with wide eyes.

"Okay," Madison said, taking a seat at one end of the rectangular-shaped mat with its four rows of green, yellow, blue, and red polka dots. "Let's go over the rules of this fun little game. As you can see from this plastic mat in front of us, it has a bunch of different colored circles. In a few moments, we're going to divide up into teams. Two partners will stand side-by-side on the four dots on one end of the mat and another team of two will stand opposite them on the other end of the mat."

She motioned to a compass-shaped device nestled between her legs with a needle pointing to the four alternating colors arranged in a circle.

"Then I'm going to spin this little needle and call out which body part each person must use to touch which colored circle. Only one body part and one person can occupy any one circle at any given time. But as you'll soon discover, the availability of circles quickly diminishes as the game advances, so you'll have to move fast to capture the circle closest to you."

"How do you decide who wins?" my friend Lily from our last camping trip asked.

"It gets harder and harder to keep yourself balanced over the mat as the players get into increasingly twisted positions," Madison said. "Whichever player or team falls first onto the mat or touches any body part other than their hand or foot loses."

"What if two people reach out and touch one of the circles at the same time?" Dylan asked.

"As the referee, I reserve the right to decide who got there first." Maddy clamped her hands together in excitement. "Are you guys ready to start?"

"How do we decide on the teams?" I asked, peering at the sexy group of men sitting opposite me. "And why are the men and women sitting on opposite sides of the mat?"

"At first, *I'll* decide who will pair up with whom. But as people get winnowed out, the winner of each round will move on until there's literally only one last man or woman standing. As for the separation of the boys and girls, the reason for that will be revealed soon enough. Shall we proceed?"

Everybody glanced around the circle excitedly at one another, then they peered toward Maddy and nodded.

"Alright then," Madison said. "Who shall we get started with?"

She panned around the group slowly, then nodded while rubbing her hands together with a mischievous grin.

"Let's mix it up a little to get started. We'll have Lily and Dylan form one group and Hannah and Brad form the other group. If you haven't yet removed your footwear, please do so now since you'll definitely want bare feet to maximize your traction on the slippery mat."

The four players stood up and took positions on opposite ends of the mat as Madison had instructed. Then she spun the needle on the game card and called out the first move.

"Okay, the first move is: left leg on a yellow circle."

The four players hesitated for a moment trying to figure out the easiest and quickest route to the designated circle, then each of them awkwardly extended their legs forward, bumping their knees and ankles against their partners' bodies. The ones who already were standing on a yellow circle only had to take one simple step forward, but their partners who were a little further away from that side of the game mat had to stretch and bend over them to reach the next available circle.

"*Oooo,*" some of the people sitting around the circle chortled, realizing how soon the game would have the participants tied up in knots.

"So far so good," Maddy said, smiling at the two teams leaned over one another. "How are you guys doing so far?"

"Piece of cake," Dylan said with his left leg hovering a few inches overtop his partner Lily's bent knee.

"I can see how there's a certain *first-mover* advantage here," Hannah nodded, watching her partner Brad grunting to hold his position stretched further out toward the center of the mat, with his head now lowered to the same level as her loose-fitting T-shirt showing her braless breasts bouncing inches away from his face.

"True," he said, smiling up at Hannah. "But the view isn't all bad."

Everybody in the group chuckled, while his wife Laura looked at him playfully with dagger eyes.

"Okay," Maddy said, returning her attention to the spinner. "Let's ramp up the degree of difficulty a little bit."

She spun the needle once again, and it stopped on a new color.

"This time," she said. "You need to touch a green circle with your right hand."

The players quickly scanned the game mat to decipher

the easiest way of getting to the nearest dot, then they lurched forward, bending and bumping against their partners to reach the designated target. Once again, it was a fairly simple move for Hannah to reach only one circle forward and to her right, while her partner Brad had to reach all the way to the opposite side of the mat overtop of both his knee and Hannah's to reach diagonally across the game board.

By the time all four players had twisted their bodies to successfully reach the intended target, both teams had become further entangled, with their crotches rubbing up against their partners legs and hips, and their heads pressed up tightly against their torsos. I noticed a fair-sized bulge in the crotch of Brad's tight sweat pants, but I wasn't sure if he was becoming aroused from all the suggestive moves and rubbing of body parts, or if he was just a little better hung than most of the other guys. I peered over at his wife Laura and noticed her giving him a devilish smile while staring at his tumescent package. Either she was giving him tacit encouragement to rub whatever body parts came in contact, or they had already discussed the possibility of the game taking a 'swinger' turn.

"Ohh!" the group murmured in appreciation as they watched the players move into tighter and more stretched positions. Both Dylan and Brad were puffing more heavily now as they struggled to hold their newly strained positions, having deferred to their female partners to give them the easier first-mover advantage.

"*That* looks a little more interesting," Madison nodded approvingly while peering at each of the players. "I hope you guys have been working out at the gym, because it's only going to get more difficult from here on."

"No sweat," Dylan said, grunting to hold his position.

"That's not what the beads of perspiration on your forehead are telling me," Maddy smiled. "I hope you're all wearing sturdy clothing, because we're about to test the strength of your seams with this next move."

She spun the needle again and this time it landed on the red color.

"Now you have to touch a red circle with your–"

She paused, giving everyone a moment to prepare for their next move.

"*Left* hand!"

This time, Hannah had to reach overtop of Brad's bent leg to reach the circle closest to her, while he had to twist his body facing up to reach his left hand all the way to the other side of the mat. By the time they both had rested their limbs on the designated markers, Hannah was leaning overtop of his crab-shaped body, with her dangling tits rubbing against the rapidly bulging bump in his sweatpants.

For his part, since he was already positioned on the red side of the mat, Dylan only had to reach one circle forward to place his hand on the board. But this time, his partner Lily had the tougher stretch, having to lean over his back to reach the last red dot between the two men's hands. With her body hunched forward into a doggy-style position, it looked like she was humping Dylan's butt with her crotch.

"Woo-hoo!" the group cheered at the erotic ways the two couples had chosen to position themselves.

"Well that certainly looks like fun," Maddy said, raising a playful eyebrow. "Are you guys starting to enjoy yourselves yet?"

"That's one way of putting it," Brad huffed while struggling to hold his upturned position with Hannah resting her body on his hips to support herself.

"I could hold this position for *hours*," Dylan kidded as

Lily rubbed her crotch against his ass in their bent-over positions.

The group chuckled, but I noticed Laura shifting her position awkwardly as she watched her husband get increasingly turned on rubbing his thickening rod against Hannah's swinging tits.

"We'll have to see about that," Madison snickered as she spun the game needle one more time a little more forcefully.

After spinning around four or five times, it finally landed on a green circle again.

"Your next move," Madison announced with a glimmer in her eye, is to move your right leg to a green circle," she announced.

The four players peered down at the mat then back up at Maddy with a puzzled expression.

"But all the green circles are already occupied," Hannah said. "What do we do now?"

"In this instance," Maddy said. "Two people may occupy the same circle, but only with their own partner, not someone from the opposing team."

The players paused for a moment trying to determine how they could reach around everyone's twisted body parts, then Brad stepped his foot forward two circles, resting it beside Hannah's downturned hand. The action pressed his crotch even tighter against Hannah's compressed tits, and she caressed his little toe playfully with her index finger while he struggled to hold his position.

But this time it was Dylan's turn to be put into an increasingly difficult position. He had to move his right foot in front of his left leg on the same plane, while Lily had to simultaneous reach forward with her own right foot, trying to place it beside his. With her full weight already boring down on top of Dylan's back, and with his legs no longer in a spread position to balance himself, the two players quickly toppled onto the mat in a jumble of limbs.

"Nooo!" the crowded roared in laughter while Dylan and Lily embraced each other, completely exhausted.

"We appear to have a winner," Madison nodded, motioning for Hannah and Brad to extricate themselves from their twisted position. "You two can relieve yourselves now if you'd like. Although it looks like you're kind of enjoying yourselves in that position, so if you need to take a moment to compose yourselves, don't let me rush you."

"Mmm," Hannah purred, smiling at Brad prostrated beneath her with an arched back. "I wouldn't mind taking advantage of my partner in his currently vulnerable position, but something tells me his wife would prefer we separate before one of us gets some other ideas."

"Don't let me get in the way of your fun," she said, winking at Brad with a sly smile. "It's all part of the game. Whatever happens at Madison's place *stays* at Madison's place. Isn't that right, honey?"

"I suppose so," Brad grunted. "But I'm not sure I can hold this position much longer. Perhaps I should save my strength for the next round if this means the two of us will be moving on."

"Actually," Madison smiled with a devilish grin. "Only *one* of you will be moving on to the next round. I have a slightly *different* idea for how to make the next step it a little more interesting."

As Hannah and Brad untangled themselves and lifted themselves off the mat, they looked at Maddy with a suspicious expression. They undoubtedly were thinking the same thing the rest of us were regarding Madison's email instruction to wash our bodies thoroughly in preparation for the event, intimating that we would soon be intermingling our bodies without clothes in subsequent rounds.

The only question now was who would be volunteered to join with whom, and would it be with the men or the women? As I contemplated all the combinations and permutations, I watched Brad resume his position at the other side of the mat while crossing his legs and folding his hands over his crotch to conceal the swelling in his sweat pants. Meanwhile, the growing wetness between my *own* legs suggested I wasn't quite done with the idea of playing a slightly different version of this 'twist and groan' game with the opposite sex after all.

3

———

After the two teams sat back down and everybody had their wine glasses topped up, Maddy continued with her instructions for the next round.

"So, as you can see," she smiled. "This game has a tendency to get you tied up into some pretty imaginative, close-contact positions. I thought to make it even more interesting in the next round we might try it without clothes..."

Some people from both sides of the mat began darting their eyes around the circle, already thinking about who they hoped to get hooked up with.

"I know most of you pretty well," Madison continued. "And I chose you specifically because you're pretty open-minded about these things. Some of you have already participated in a similar type of group interaction at my last nude blindfolded party game. But if any of you are hesitant to expose yourself in front of the group, you're welcome to remain clothed and sit out the action while you enjoy the rest of the show."

Most of the guys simply nodded their heads with a sly smile while I listened to the escalated breathing from the girls around me indicating their willingness to get involved.

"Is this going to be a *unisex* sort of thing or..." Marco asked, eager to mix it up with some of the girls he was eying up on the other side of the mat.

"It's funny you should mention that, Marco," Maddy grinned. "I thought to make it even more interesting, we'd do it a little differently each round. I'm thinking first we do just the girls, then just the guys, then we finish up with a mixed group. I know some of you like to swing one way or the other, so this way everybody will have a chance to mingle with their preferred partners."

"How do we decide who'll participate in each round?" Marco continued, shifting uncomfortably at the idea of getting naked and rubbing his body together with a bunch of other straight guys.

"The winners of each round will move forward of course," she said. "So Hannah moves into the next round and Brad the one after that. Plus, two more guys will move forward to the last round after it's their turn. So that'll be a little extra incentive for you to try to win your round. As for the remaining participants, that will be my choice."

Marco nodded his head and pursed his lips as he ran through the possibilities in his head.

"So for this next round, it's going to be all girls. Hannah is on deck by virtue of her team's win in the last round. And to join her, how about we have Jade and Laura..."

Maddy paused as she glanced tentatively at Shae sitting on the girls' side of the mat.

"I don't want to make any presumptions about *you*, Shae," she said. "Do you have a preference for which group you'd like to join?"

"Actually," she said with a sly grin, glancing across the mat toward the guys eyeing her curvy body greedily. "I think I'd rather join the guys if that's okay with you."

"Absolutely," Maddy said. "So then to finish up the girls' group, let's go with...*Natalie*. Are you guys all good to go?"

The four of us peered at one another with raised eyebrows, then slowly nodded in agreement.

"Okay," Madison smiled. "You know the next step then."

"Um, okay," I said, standing up to slowly unbutton my pajama top. But who will team up with who this time?"

"Good question, Jade," Maddy said, pausing to consider the most appropriate mix. "How about you and Laura form one team and Natalie and Hannah form the other?"

The four of us stood up and slowly removed our clothes, then walked tentatively toward the opposite ends of the game mat. Every single set of eyes in the room including our own, ran wildly over the sea of naked flesh, and I could feel tummy fluttering in knots knowing that soon we'd be rubbing our naked bodies together in front of the rest of the group. As I stood at one end of the game mat and placed my feet on two of the adjacent dots, Laura reached her hand out to my side and squeezed it gently. I could feel a charge of electricity shooting through me, realizing that soon I'd have a chance to molest her body with near impunity right in front of her husband, whose growing bulge in his pants was now impossible to hide.

"Alright then," Maddy said when she saw all of us standing in the starting position. "Are you guys ready?"

"Ready as we'll ever be," I said, feeling the goose bumps spreading over my entire body.

Maddy spun the game needle and it landed on a blue color.

"Your first move is: right leg to a blue circle."

Since my right leg was already resting on the first blue dot on the board, I simply had to step forward one circle. But with Laura's right foot resting two rows over on the other side of the mat, she had to reach three rows over toward me, stretching her leg over top of my thigh to reach the next blue circle. As her naked vulva grazed the top of my leg, I gasped at the sensation of her touching me with her private parts. With her legs now spread almost three feet apart, everybody who was seated at floor level could see her gaping slit exposed inches above my flesh.

On the other side of the mat, I watched Hannah step one circle forward and one to her left, while Natalie had to similarly stretch overtop of her knee to position her foot on the last blue dot next to Laura's foot. With the four of us now pressed forward against one another and our feet positioned only inches apart, we stared at each other's faces, trying not to let our eyes dart below our direct line of sight.

"Looking good, ladies!" Madison, nodded approvingly at our tight bodies flexing and straining to hold our partial squats. "Are you ready for the next move?"

"*Bring* it," Hannah joked, elbowing Natalie good-naturedly in her abdomen while pressing the side of her stomach against her firm breasts.

Madison spun the needle again and this time it landed on the red color.

"Your next move is, left hand to a red circle."

Everybody paused momentarily, trying to figure out the easiest path to the designated target. Realizing that my partner would have to reach all the way across the game board to reach a red circle, I moved one dot forward so she'd have a little more room to maneuver over my hunched body to reach the next circle. She had to squat her body quite a bit lower to reach the distance, and as she leaned her torso over my bent right leg, I felt my tits sliding across the top of her back and the wetness of her slit pressing against my upper thigh.

By the time she placed her left hand in front of mine, we were both groaning softly, partly from the strain of holding the more crunched position of our bodies, but also from the erotic sensation of feeling our intimate parts touching one another. I wasn't sure if she'd ever had sex with another woman, but I was pretty sure the slick mark she was leaving on the top of my thigh wasn't just sweat from overexertion. For his part, I noticed Brad darting his eyes over the two of us as he watched Laura's breasts dangling down in front of her with her pointed, hard nipples. The bulge in his pants was now pointing unabashedly straight up, tenting almost an entire foot, and he was no longer making much of an effort to conceal it.

At the same time, Hannah and Natalie were struggling to fill the remaining two red dots on the other end of the game board. Once again, Hannah had to move her hand only slightly forward, but with her legs already crossed from the first maneuver, by the time she placed her left hand forward of her right hand, she looked like one of those twisted donut sticks or a piece of braided rope. But Natalie had a much more difficult task trying to reach the last red circle, since it was almost five feet away from her position on the other side of the mat. She tried repeatedly to stretch to reach it, bumping her hips and breasts all over Hannah's body in the process, but it was simply too far away for her to reach.

"What do we do now?" Hannah said, peering toward Maddy in frustration. "Natalie isn't tall enough to reach the last available circle."

"Remember," Maddy smiled, obviously enjoying the

four of us stretching and rubbing our slippery bodies together trying to follow her instructions. "Two people from the same team can occupy the same circle, you don't always have to find an unoccupied one. Also, you're allowed to lift one limb temporarily to permit your partner to reach a circle, if that's the only way to achieve it."

"*Now* you tell me," Natalie joked, looking at Maddy with a mock frown. The rest of the group laughed, but I noticed the guys closer to her end of the mat were more interested in staring at her upturned ass and her glistening pussy, which was spread wide open for their viewing pleasure.

After taking a moment to discuss amongst themselves the best strategy for reaching the new target, Hannah finally lifted her right foot a few inches off the mat while Natalie hunched underneath her outstretched leg and positioned her hand on the same red dot that Hannah was occupying. By the time they were finished, Natalie was precariously balanced in a low squat position with her pussy mere inches off the mat and Hannah's bare mound pressing against the side of her torso with her tits pressed firmly against the small of her back.

I noticed the plastic mat underneath Natalie's pussy was glistening with a shiny film, and I wasn't sure if it was from the sweat dripping off her body or from her slit dripping in excitement from all the interbody rubbing and the lascivious stares of both the men and women sitting around the board looking on in fascination. One thing was for certain though. Judging by the universal tenting of the guys' loose-fitting sweatpants and the squishing sound of the women shifting their weight on the floor next to me, everybody was enjoying the show tremendously.

"Wow," Maddy said, shaking her head in surprise. "You

guys are really showing great teamwork. Do you think you've got enough energy left for another tough move?"

"The *stretchier* the better," Laura purred, rocking her wet pussy against my tensing thigh as she pretended to adjust her position to support herself. Between the sensation of her humping my leg and the feeling of my erect nipples caressing the soft skin on her overturned back, I was getting just as turned on as she was, and I wondered if the spectators on my end of the mat had noticed the trickle of lubrication running down the insides of my thighs.

"Alright then," Maddy nodded. "Here goes..."

She spun the needle once again with a hard flick, and it turned around the card a few times, finally landing on a yellow circle.

"Your next move is–left hand, yellow."

The four of us looked at the board then peered up at Maddy with a confused look.

"But our left hands are already on the *red* circles," I said. "Are we allowed to move them?"

"Of course," Madison said. "You only have to stay on a designated circle until the spinner shows a new position."

Natalie was the first person to move, relieved to have a chance to reposition her left hand closer to her side of the mat and reduce the tension on her straining quads and shoulder muscles from having to crunch down so low and spread her entire weight over the board. This time, it was Hannah's turn to twist further toward her partner as she moved her left hand from the right side of the mat toward the side closer to Natalie. In the process, the two girls ended up mashing their tits together with their faces right next to one another. Not missing an opportunity to give the rest of the group a little show, they locked lips and groaned loudly while rolling their erect nipples together.

Whether they were doing it out of fun or because they were genuinely turned on by the tight connection of their intimate parts, it certainly emboldened Laura and me to ramp up the action on our end of the mat to try to match their performance. Fortunately, the new hand placement afforded both of us a chance to relieve some of the tension in our bodies, with Laura moving her hand closer to her side of the board. But with my legs already crossed over one another, I had reach over the side of her overturned back to position my left hand diagonally across her body. By the time I was finished, I could feel the muscles of her buttocks pressing hard against my mound, and I reached my free hand around the side of her back to squeeze her perky breasts and pinch her nipples.

"Mmm," she purred as she humped my pussy with her ass while I felt her up. "Are you sure we have to move one more time?" she asked Madison. "Because I'm kind of digging this position."

"Well I'll be happy to give you guys a little longer if you need a moment to pause," Maddy smiled. "But something tells me that the boys are getting a bit restless over there on the other side of the mat. We better keep the action moving before they blow a gasket or something. You girls are certainly giving everybody plenty of food for thought in terms of experimenting with new positions, wouldn't you agree, guys?"

"Absolutely," Taylor gushed, as she watched me trib the side of Laura's ass with my wet pussy.

"Mmm-hmm," Shae nodded, revealing a sizeable stiffy of her own bulging to the side of her brightly colored leotard.

"Okay, let's see what *other* creative positions you can invent," Maddy said, spinning the game needle one more time. When it finished turning, this time it pointed toward a green circle.

"Your next move is with your left leg onto a green dot."

The four of us looked at one another, then shook our heads trying to figure out how we were going to make this one work. For Laura, it was a fairly simple maneuver. She could have easily crossed her left leg over her right leg and squatted a little lower to reach the nearest circle. But for me, it was going to be considerably more difficult reaching all the way over to the opposite side of the board, especially with my right knee already pressing up tightly against my stomach. We glanced at one another, then Laura winked at me with a sly smile.

"You said we can lift one or more limbs to permit the movement of another partner, right?" she called out to Madison.

"Well *technically*," Maddy said. "I said you could lift one limb, but under the circumstances, I suppose we can give you a little more latitude..."

Laura smiled at me, then lifted her left hand and right leg one at a time until she flipped her body all the way around with her breasts now pointing up and her two knees spread apart in an arched position directly underneath me. I took one look at her splayed legs and dripping pussy, then studied the board to determine how I could best adjust my position to achieve maximum contact with her while still placing my limbs on the required spots.

After a few moments of contemplation, I decided to turn my body around a hundred and eighty degrees, so that I was now facing away from her with my ass pointed directly toward her pussy. Then I threaded one foot over her right thigh to place it back on my previously occupied blue dot, and snaked my other foot under her other leg to place my left foot on the green dot next to hers. As I leaned over to place my left hand back on the last red circle, I lowered my pelvis toward her until our pussies melded together in a slippery scissors position.

"Ohhh!" I could hear some of the women sitting beside us gasp as they watched us grind our vulvas together while we pretended to exert ourselves holding the strange reverse squat position. Meanwhile, the men simply groaned as they stared at our wet pussies while they rubbed their legs together, desperate to give their aching hard-ons some much needed direct stimulation.

Hannah and Natalie regarded us with amusement for a few seconds, then not to be outdone, they tried to simulate a similar maneuver on their end of mat. But with both of them already in a more precarious position to begin with, first Hannah, then Natalie, attempted to stretch their elongated bodies across the board to reach the last available green circles, but they bumped into each other and fell over.

"Wooo!" the crowd cheered boisterously, impressed at Laura's and my inventiveness pulling off the tricky maneuver.

But with the round technically over, neither one of us was in a hurry to stop the sexy grinding of our pussies in full view of the rest of the group. And with Brad nodding enthusiastically at us while stroking his dick under his sweats, Laura lifted her head towards mine and we kissed passionately while grunting and moaning from the mutual pleasure building between our connected thighs.

Within seconds, both of us had a powerful climax connected together in our erotic position as we hummed loudly into each other's mouths while jerking our hips together in a mutual spasm. As usual, I made a bigger mess than usual, squirting all over the mat when I came, causing the guys' eyeballs to almost pop out of their heads. After we both finished coming, we plopped back down onto the sticky mat, pressing our nipples and breasts together while we embraced each other in a soft hug.

"Wow," Maddy said after a long pause. "That was certainly an *exciting* finish to this round. I don't know about *you* guys, but I'm already chomping at the bit to see some more action in the next round."

She peered over at the lineup of guys sitting at the side of the mat with sheepish looks on their faces and raging hard-ons poking up out of their pants.

"How about it, boys–are you up for a little grinding and drooling of your own?"

"Oh, we're *up* for it all right," Shae said, standing up as she pulled down her leotard to reveal an eight-inch throbbing erection pointing straight up toward the ceiling.

4
____

After Laura and I took a moment to compose ourselves, we all distracted ourselves cleaning off the slippery mat, then Maddy refreshed our glasses of wine for the third time. By now, all of us were feeling tipsy enough to lose whatever inhibitions we might have previously had about getting naked in front of the group. When we all sat back down around the game board in preparation for round three, I noticed the boys were still sporting partial woodies in their loose-fitting sweats.

Whether it was because they were still turned on from watching Laura and me rubbing our pussies together or because they were looking forward to getting up close and personal with Shae in the next round was unclear. Although she definitely had a man's equipment down below, as a female-identifying transgender person, she otherwise had a beautiful feminine figure, with firm natural-looking breasts, a narrow waist, and long, slender legs. Plus, she was abso-lutely gorgeous to boot, with full lips, high cheekbones, and large, brown doe-eyes. On top of all that, she was an absolute *minx* in the sack, as my fluttering pussy reminded me from our last time together.

Whoever Maddy chose to join her with in the next round was in for a pleasant surprise.

"Alright, then," she said, resuming her position at the end of the game mat with the spinner card nestled between her crossed legs. "We're going to move on to the boys' round now, or should I more correctly say–" smiling in Shae's direction, "the *open* round.

"Brad's up first, by virtue of his win in the first round. And Shae has also generously volunteered to join the group. And since Marco's already expressed his eagerness to get in on the action, why don't you join this group too?"

Then she paused as she scanned the remaining three men.

"And to round out the group of four, let's have...Dylan."

I smiled when I heard Maddy's choice of players for the next round. Although Marco and Brad appeared to be straight-as-an-arrow heterosexuals, I knew from previous experience that Dylan was unabashedly bisexual, and that Shae would swing whichever way the wind was blowing.

And something told me there'd be a little more than *wind* blowing in this next round.

"So, if you guys are ready," Madison smiled. "Assume the positions."

"*Naked?*" Marco said, still not entirely comfortable with the idea of rubbing his body against a bunch of other nude guys.

"Of course," Maddy said. "That's more than half the fun. Of course, if you'd rather *sit out* this round, I can't guarantee you'll be chosen in the last round..."

Marco peered across the game board at Shae who had

already fully disrobed, staring at her gorgeous figure and her swelling, half-erect dick.

"Um, no, it's fine," he said, beginning to pull off his t-shirt. "I mean it's not going to be *all* boys this time around..."

Madison simply smiled and nodded while the rest of the men removed their gym togs then paused at the side of the mat with their pendulous dicks throbbing in anticipation of the next move.

"Who'll be joining with *who* this time?" Brad asked, his body language also revealing a certain degree of unease standing next to three bouncing cocks on his side of the mat.

"I suppose it doesn't really matter, does it?" Maddy smirked, knowing full well the men would soon lose their inhibitions once the round got underway. "Let's have you and Shae on one team, and Marco and Dylan on the other."

Brad nodded his head and smiled, relieved to be paired with the sexy transgender girl rather than one of the guys at the opposite end of the game board. For his part, Marco simply frowned, refusing to look at his partner, who had a curious grin on his face.

This should be interesting, I thought, noticing everyone's peckers slowly inflating and lengthening over their tight balls. All four of the players had well-toned bodies and beautiful penises with trimmed bushes and shaved balls. *Straight, my ass*, I thought, noticing Marco's dick slowly rising in spite of his best attempt to hold it down with his covered hands.

Brad and Shae stepped up to one end of the game mat, while Marco and Dylan stood side-by-side on the opposite end. While the three men stared stoically straight ahead at each other's faces, Shae shamelessly darted her eyes up and down each of their figures with a big Cheshire Cat grin on her face.

"Are you guys ready?" Maddy asked.

"Oh, I think we're *ready*, alright," Shae smiled.

Madison spun the game card and the needle landed on a yellow color.

"Okay," she said. "Your first move is with your left hand to a yellow circle."

With all the dots open beyond the four at each end of the game mat, the first move was always the easiest. Since Dylan was already standing on a yellow circle, he only had to twist his torso forty-five degrees to place his hand on the nearest dot. But because Marco was standing slightly further away and had to reach forward to the next unoccupied circle, he had to extend his arm over top of Dylan's, lowering his head to the same level as his midsection. With their bare skin touching for the first time, I noticed Dylan's member twitching between his legs. As the only uncircumcised member of the group, Marco couldn't help staring at it hanging only a few inches away from his face.

On the other side of the game board, Brad and Shae peered at one another before they took their first move, discussing who would go where. It was nice to see them collaborating right out of the gate, and I wasn't sure if it was because Brad was just trying to be polite with his ladylike partner, or because he was hoping she'd take the initiative in bringing them into closer contact. After a few seconds, Shae motioned for him to bend over and move one circle forward, then she twisted her body and leaned over his back, placing her hand on the last available yellow circle in the middle of the board.

The move forced her pelvis onto the side of Brad's angled knee, with her plump tits rubbing against the top of his back. It hadn't taken long for her to regain her full erection, and at eight-inches-plus in length, it flapped up against the underside of his thigh as he tried to maintain his composure staring towards the other players, similarly bent over. But I noticed Laura, who'd chosen to sit next to me to watch the rest of the proceedings, was watching her husband's physical reaction carefully as she resting her palms between her crossed legs. When he glanced briefly over at her, she spread her legs further apart for him to see her glistening pussy while she rubbed the fingers of her right hand softly over her clit. Within seconds, Brad's big pole lengthened until it was almost touching the floor.

"You *did* say that any body part other than our hands or feet touching the mat would disqualify us, right?" he said to Madison, somewhat chagrined at his inability to hold his libido in check under the full gaze of the other participants in the group.

"Well, *yes*," Maddy smiled, noticing his huge, stiffening erection. "But under the circumstances, I think I'll make an exception for certain–er–*autonomous* appendages. I'm just happy you guys seem to be enjoying yourselves so early in the round. Shall we ramp up the action with the next move?"

"By all means," Brad said, staring at his wife's pussy while she played with her clit watching Shae rub her stiffy along the soft hairs on the underside of his thigh.

Madison spun the needle again, and this time it landed on a green dot.

"Your next turn," she said, "is with your left leg to a green circle."

With Dylan already standing on a green dot, it would have been a fairly simple maneuver for him to step one circle forward. But knowing that it would be a far more diffi-

cult for his partner to reach all the way across the board
with his left leg, he chose instead to move two circles
forward, which necessitated Marco reaching underneath his
bent-over torso and upturned ass, directly under his
swinging balls and rapidly growing dick. Marco tried his
best to achieve the maneuver without touching his partner's
skin, but with their hands already planted directly on the
floor in front of one another and their bodies hunched over
close to the surface of the mat, it was impossible for him to
snake his leg under Dylan without grazing his balls and
flapping dick.

I smiled at Dylan's ingenuity in forcing the direct body
contact with his partner, recognizing that he was deter-
mined to force Marco to touch their body parts at one point
or another. As Marco struggled to hold his awkward three-
point position with his upper thigh quivering against his
partner's bouncing pole, I noticed the pink head of Dylan's
cock begin to emerge from the end of his foreskin, revealing
his growing excitement from the touch of his reluctant
partner.

On the other end of the board, Brad and Shae took
another moment to plan their strategy then they nodded at
one another and Brad stepped two circles forward and one
diagonal, exposing his shaved balls and anus to the rest of
the group and his partner, with his now fully erect penis
flapping up against his belly. Just like Marco, Shae had to
make an equally strenuous stretch to move her left leg all
the way to the other side of the mat. In the process, she had
to twist her hips and torso almost one-hundred-and-eighty
degrees, placing her penis and balls directly in contact with
Brad's. By this point, they were staring directly into each
other's faces and for a moment, there was an awkward

silence as everybody wondered how the two of them would react from their intimate contact.

"How are you guys doing over there?" Madison said, trying to break the awkward tension in the room. "Cause, uh, from this angle at least, it looks like your arms and legs aren't the *only* body parts getting a little workout there."

"Well, I've never been in this kind of situation before," Brad said with an embarrassed flush on his face. "You know what they say about the little head having a mind of its own. I don't exactly have full control over these things."

"So I *see*," Maddy nodded. "But I'm not quite sure I'd call that your *little* head."

Then she turned her attention to Marco, who was trying to hold his position while maintaining minimum intimate contact between his and Dylan's equally tumescent body parts.

"How about you, Marco and Dylan? Are you guys managing to navigate your way around each other's dangling participles in that convoluted position?"

"This is harder than it looks," Marco panted.

"So I can *see*," Maddy smiled, staring at his hard poker, now pointing straight up between Dylan's splayed legs, only inches away from his face. Don't let us interfere with your fun if you want to take a few moments to enjoy yourselves in your currently advantageous positions. We're all big boys and girls here. None of us are going to judge if you want to grab the bull by the horns, in a manner of speaking. Am I right, gang?"

"Damn *straight*," Laura said, beginning to jill her clit more vigorously as she watched her husband's and Shae's big cocks bobbing against one another.

"Fuck, yeah," Jake nodded, stroking his dick under his sweats as he stared at the four twitching hard-ons mere inches away from his face. "This is *way* hotter than I ever imagined when I played this game as a kid."

"Speaking of," Maddy said, trying to encourage the two teams to abandon their final reservations. "Haven't we *all* experimented a little bit with our same sex when we were younger? The only difference now is that it's no longer taboo, and we're surrounded by like-minded friends."

Dylan took one look at Marco's twitching hard-on poking up between his open legs, then peered over at his partner to gauge his readiness to proceed to the next level. Marco was too shy to give direct verbal assent, but the look of lust on his face was more than enough for Dylan to take the next step. Without hesitating any further, he lowered his head and began sucking on Marco's flaring bulb with a loud slopping sound. Marco threw his head back and pressed his hips upward, forcing his dick further into her partner's mouth.

When you're horny and someone's sucking on your dick, I smiled, *everyone's gay at one point or another.* I uncrossed my legs in sympathy with Laura and thrust two fingers into my sopping slit, egging them on even further.

With Marco giving his unconscious approval to engage more intimately with his partner, Brad and Shae seemed to take this as a sign that all bets were off and that anything was fair game at this point. Without missing a beat, Shae tilted her head up towards Brad and he bent down and kissed her passionately on the lips. As they grunted into each other's mouths, Shae reached between their stomachs with her free hand and wrapped it around their connected poles as they both began humping her hand vigorously.

"Oh my *God*," Laura moaned watching her husband frotting his big dick with Shae while she rubbed her tits against his chiseled pecs. "Yes baby," she purred. "Fuck her gorgeous cock. I want to watch you cream all over her tits."

By now, virtually everybody around the game mat either had their hands stuffed down their pants or had pulled off their clothing and were madly jerking and jilling themselves taking in the erotic action at both ends of the mat. With Dylan using his well-practiced technique to expertly suck off his partner, it didn't take long for Marco's breathing and groaning to reach a crescendo as Dylan deep-throated him down to his balls while caressing his perineum with the fingers of his free hand.

"*Oh fuck, oh fuck...*" Marco panted. "I'm going to come! Fuck, I'm going to *come!*"

With one last powerful thrust of his hips into Dylan's mouth and a loud grunt, his hips suddenly began shaking as his buttocks trembled while he emptied his seed into Dylan's mouth. It seemed to take almost a full minute for him to stop grunting and shaking as Dylan calmly swallowed his load.

I smiled realizing he'd probably never experienced a blow-job like that ever before.

Meanwhile, watching the erotic scene play out between their opposing partners seemed to embolden Brad and Shae to ramp up the action at their own end of the mat. Listening to his wife egging him on and seeing her fingering her pussy while she watched them rub their big dicks together had a similar effect on Brad. A long string of pre-cum dangled down from the tip of his hard-on, and the extra lubrication made a sexy slurping sound as Shae squeezed their two dicks harder together.

"Mmmft!" the two of them groaned with their faces joined together in a vice-grip as they thrust their tongues into each other's mouths. By now, they were humping each other wildly, and I could see their purple heads popping in and out of Shae's fist as the fingers in her hand got redder and redder while she gripped their poles more tightly. With both of their dicks considerably larger than most men's, she could barely get her hand half way around their joined organs, and this simply added to the excitement of the moment.

With both of them nearing the height of their pleasure, Laura and I both pounded our pussies with our fingers, spreading our legs ever wider as we neared our own orgasms. When Shae and Brad suddenly began jetting long streams of cum all over the mat in front of them between her clenched hand, the two of us squealed in delight as we both gushed our juices in front of us onto the mat, jerking in unison with the couple directly in front of us.

While all this was going on, I was so lost in my *own* pleasure and those of the players on the mat, I hardly even noticed everybody else around the board jerking and moaning in mutual ecstasy while they took in the incredible view of everybody climaxing simultaneously. Glancing briefly over in Madison's direction, I noticed that even *she* had her hand down the front of her pants while jilling her clit, mesmerized by the orgy of activity all around her.

It only took two spins, I smiled to myself as my contractions slowly began to subside. *Two spins, for the self-styled straight boys to lose their inhibitions and get their freak on. What can possibly happen in the in the final round?*

5

———

After everybody climaxed around the game board, there was some awkward silence in the room while the four players lay in a heap on the game board. After a few minutes, Maddy stood up and brushed herself off for dramatic effect.

"Well, *that* was certainly a little more stimulating than I imagined," she smiled. "I don't know about *you* guys, but I'm kind of hungry after all that exercise. Who wants to join me in the kitchen to help put together some snacks before our final round?"

A few of the girls raised their hands while the boys shifted their equipment awkwardly, looking at their stained sweatpants.

"If the rest of you need to clean up, there's one washroom on the main floor and two upstairs. Maybe you can bring down some extra towels to clean up the game board."

Madison peered at the slick plastic mat and grimaced.

"Cause, um, I'm pretty sure there's nowhere safe to step on it right now."

Everybody chuckled, then the group separated to

prepare for the next round. When we all reassembled around the mat a half hour later, everyone seemed to have regained their composure, munching noisily on nachos and popcorn. After drinking a couple more glasses of wine, we had a pretty good buzz on again, and Maddy reached over to place the Twister spinner card back between her legs.

"Are you guys ready for the big finale?" she grinned.

"Absolutely," Jake chimed in, eager to get in on the action. "But if I'm doing the math right, I've counted a total of five winners from the three previous rounds, but only four available spots on the board?"

"Good catch," Maddy nodded. "Hannah and Brad won the first round, Jade and Laura won the second, then Brad and Shae somehow managed to stay on their feet in the last one. And we can't have an uneven number of participants if everyone's going to team up again. So, to make this last round a little more entertaining, I thought we'd add one more player and have *three* teams instead of two. It will be a little more challenging to twist around the extra bodies, but it'll also provide even more opportunities for group interaction. Are you guys up for changing it up a little in the final round?"

"Okay..." Jake continued, looking around the circle at the people who still hadn't participated in the game. "That definitely sounds more interesting, but that still leaves six of us on the sidelines. When will the *rest* of us have a turn?"

"That's a good point, Jake," Madison nodded. "But as you may have noticed from the last round, being on the sidelines doesn't mean you have to miss out on all the action. I would encourage the *rest* of you to join up in whatever way strikes your imagination so you can have just as much fun as the players on the board."

Jake darted his eyes around the circle, noticing the rest

of the attendees glancing at one another as they nodded in agreement. With four boys and two girls still unaccounted for, there'd still be plenty of opportunities to mix it up amongst the group.

"So that just leaves the matter of who'll join the other five players who've earned the right to move on," Madison said. "Since we already have four girls in the group, I think we should have one more guy to balance it out a little bit. That will also help balance out the rest of the group looking on from the sidelines. Since I'm pretty sure just about everybody else got off one way or the other in that last round, I think it's only fair that we invite Dylan back up on the board for this final round. What do you say, Dylan–are you up for another turn?"

"I never really went *down* after that last encounter," he said, pointing to his still swollen member leaning against the side of his upper thigh.

The rest of the group chuckled, admiring his impressive package.

"Okay," Madison said. "We're going to line everybody up a little differently this time with the two extra players. I was thinking about the best way to do this while we were working in the kitchen. If you guys can take your position one at a time on the board as I call your name, it'll minimize the confusion."

Everybody looked at Maddy with a puzzled expression, curious to see what she had in mind.

"First up," she said, "I'd like Brad to stand on one end of the mat with his feet on the two middle circles."

Brad dutifully walked over to his designated position, then peered at Madison with a wrinkled forehead.

Don't worry, beautiful, I smiled, peering at his retracted penis. *I'm pretty sure we'll be ironing out those wrinkles pretty soon.*

"Next up," Madison smiled, "I'd like Jade to stand on the next set of circles directly in front of Brad, facing away from him."

I jumped off the mat and took my position, playfully wagging my butt over Brad's flagging dick.

"Now let's have Shae stand in front of Jade in the same manner."

As Shae took her position on the board, I began to nod at Maddy's devious plan. With each of us lined up boy-girl in a daisy chain pattern, there would be an almost infinite number of ways for each of us to connect once we began to stretch into position.

"Now on the *other* end of the board," Madison continued. "I'd like first Hannah, then Dylan, then Laura to take similar positions facing the other three."

After everybody had taken their place on the game mat, we all peered at one another and smiled. I could feel Brad's dick already beginning to press against my ass as he got excited pondering the possibilities, especially with his wife directly facing him and Shae. I wasn't sure if this was their first swinging affair, but *one* thing was for certain. They probably didn't imagine in a million years that both of them would end up hooking up with a sexy transgender girl in the space of a single night.

"Okay," Madison said, nodding approvingly at the lineup of contestants on the board. "Do you guys think you can make this work?"

"It's going to be a little tougher to find an open spot to place all our hands and legs," Dylan said.

"True," Madison smiled. "But look at it this way. There's also going to be a lot more open 'spots' to place a few *other* things, if you catch my drift. Plus, this time, I'm going to allow multiple people to place their limbs on any one circle."

"Oh, I'm pretty sure the mood's gonna strike," Laura smirked, ogling Shae's elevating dick, only a few inches in front of her belly.

"I hope so," Maddy said. "Let's see if we can set a new record for group interaction in this final round. Here we go..."

She flicked the needle with her middle finger, and after a few spins it landed on a red dot.

"Your first move," she announced, "is to a red circle with your right hand. But since one team is pointed in the opposite direction on the board, I'm going to allow Hannah's team to move their hands to the other side of mat onto a green circle."

Everybody paused for a moment, realizing they had a little more latitude as to who could go where. I saw the wheels turning in the other team's heads as they tried to plan how best to configure their bodies to take maximum advantage of everybody's rapidly swelling body parts.

Shae was the first person to move as she reached one circle forward and one to her right, bringing her face down to the same level as Laura's pussy directly in front of her. Seeing Shae's sexy ass pointing up in the air in front of me, I moved next, placing my hand directly on top of hers, causing my breasts to press atop her back. With two sexy girls bent over in front of him, Brad decided the best way for him to gain maximum contact would be to reach one circle forward, causing him to bend forward just enough to angle his now fully erect spear atop the small of my back. Shae and I hummed in approval at the feeling of our partners' intimate parts touching our tingling skin.

With Laura watching how the three of us had chosen to arrange ourselves, she placed her hand on her chin and massaged it slowly, crafting her plan. While the two others behind her waited for her to make the next move, she surprised all of us when she arched her body backwards, placing her palm on the green dot opposite Hannah's foot at her end of the board. It was definitely a more challenging position to put herself in than she might have otherwise performed, but it forced her knees further forward to balance herself, pressing her dripping pussy even closer to Shae's downturned face.

Seeing Laura prostrated beneath him in her inverted crab position made it easy for Dylan to choose the next move, and he smiled as he reached for the green circle opposite her midsection, causing his erect organ to point directly down over her upturned face. With Hannah having the last move, she glanced at Dylan's tight balls hanging between his legs, then reached two circles forward to rest her hand beside his as she proceeded to dry-hump him from behind.

"Looks like things are unfolding very nicely," Madison purred, nodding her head at the ingenious way each of us had chosen to arrange ourselves to maximize contact with our preferred partners. "I don't know how long some of you are going to be able to hold those positions, but it's certainly going to be interesting to see where the game play takes us next."

Without any further hesitation, she spun the needle again, and it landed on a green circle. I could see from my bent-over vantage point that the needle pointed toward our right hand again, but after noticing how carefully we'd all arranged our bodies to bring our private parts closer together, she decided to create a new instruction.

"This time," she said, "Brad's team will move their left leg to a green circle and Hannah's team will likewise move their left leg to the opposite side to a red circle."

This time it was Laura who made the first move, as she quickly repositioned her left foot one dot sideways to rebalance her weight and relieve the strain on her arm extended behind her. As she watched Laura's pretty pussy opening up in front of her face, Shae moved next, moving her left leg forward to the opposite side of Laura's hips, placing the tip of her bobbing cock directly in contact with her glistening slit.

"Mmm," Laura groaned, trying to push her hips further forward to take Shae's wand in her hole. But with her body already in a fully stretched position, she had limited freedom of movement. If anything more exciting were to happen between the two of them, it would have to be *Shae* taking the initiative. Instead, she simply peered at Laura with a sexy grin, and rocked her hips from side to side, dripping precum over the insides of Laura's thighs.

As he watched his wife moaning in delirious frustration, Brad's hard-on pressed harder into the small of my back, and he stepped forward two steps to place his left foot on the green circle next to my shoulder. With his hot balls pressing up against the back of my ass, I paused trying to decipher the best way to bring us closer together. It would have been easier for me to stretch my left leg forward only one dot, but that would have angled my ass further down toward the mat and out of reach of his throbbing organ. Instead, I threaded my leg under his bent knee and placed my foot directly behind me, next to his on the green circle. By so doing, I tilted my ass further up in the air, and he pulled his hips back a few inches, letting his organ flap down under my quivering slit.

Meanwhile, with Dylan staring at the tempting combination of Shae's hard-on probing Laura's upturned pussy and her tits staring him in the face, he stretched his leg one dot sideways to the nearest red circle. In so doing, he lowered his balls onto Laura's face, whereupon she began licking the sensitive area between his testicles and his anus.

"Uhnn," he groaned, enjoying the combination of the erotic show on display in front of him and Laura's teasing of his perineum.

Once again, Hannah had the final-move advantage, having seen how everybody else had arranged themselves. Realizing her only chance to gain any direct stimulation on her throbbing clit would be to grind her pussy against his tailbone, she leaned forward two circles, placing her left foot beside Dylan's as she began to make a wet slick mark rubbing herself against his ass.

"*That's* what I'm talking about," Maddy panted, getting just as worked up as the rest of the group watching the players on the mat move into a tighter formation and beginning to rub their bodies together. I noticed some of the other viewers had already begun to reach over and start caressing one another. I smiled, knowing that it wouldn't just be the players mixing it up on the game board who'd have a chance to hookup and get off.

"I'm not even sure you guys are going to be able to *make* another move stretched out the way you are overtop of one another," Madison smiled. "This is beginning to look a little more like a game of *K'Nex* than Twister, with everybody looking ready to plug each other's holes. But let's give it one more try to see where the spinner will take us next..."

Madison spun the needle again and glanced down at it only briefly before turning her attention back to the game board to decipher the best way to consummate our tentative connections. After a few moments, and without even bothering to consult the position of the needle, she called out the last instruction.

"Your next move, if you can pull it off, is with your right leg to a red circle for Brad's team and right leg to a *green* circle for Hannah's team."

I looked down at the board and smiled, realizing that Maddy was instructing us to spread our legs even wider apart, giving our partners easier access to our waiting holes. By now, Brad's huge prick had extended all the way up the underside of my stomach to my belly button, and eager to feel his full manhood buried inside me, I shifted my right leg directly to the side, placing it next to his hand on the mat. By so doing, I tilted my pussy further upward in the direction of his tight balls. Fortunately, he only had to shift his foot over one circle so that he was now perfectly balanced over my quivering ass. I reached between both of our legs and pointed his throbbing pole into my dripping slit, and he slowly began to slide it inside me. I groaned as it began to fill me up while Laura tilted her head up and moaned along with me seeing her husband fuck me from behind.

"Yeah, baby," she purred. "Fuck Jade's sweet pussy. Make her squirt all over Shae's beautiful ass while I suck on her tits."

"*Fuck* yes," Brad groaned as he watched Shae shift her right leg one row sideways and behind her so she'd have better leverage to plow his wife's pussy. Eager to facilitate the connection, Laura also shifted her leg over one row so that she was now perfectly balanced in an upside-down position with her pussy spread far apart directly in front of Shae's flapping cock. She wasted no time inserting her throbbing prick into Laura's hole, burying it up to her balls.

As she began to hump Laura in her bent over position, Laura sucked loudly on her hard nipples, groaning in pleasure along with the rest of the bystanders who were getting increasingly bold touching one another at the edge of the mat.

By this point, Dylan was just about ready to burst a gasket having observed the erotic act unfolding before him twice now with no direct stimulation on his part. As he watched Shae's tongue dancing over Laura's tits directly below his cock, he pressed his right leg forward and one row sideways, shifting his weight forward just enough for poke Shae in the forehead with his raging hard-on. Not skipping a beat, Shae immediately engulfed his organ in her mouth while she continued fucking Laura, prostrated beneath her.

Seeing everybody else now connected together, and with no way to fill her own streaming pussy with any warm object, Hannah shifted her right leg one circle over to her side so that she was now riding Dylan's ass like she was on a horse. With her right hand resting on the mat beside Dylan's lurching body, she reached around with her other free hand and grasped his cock hard in her fist, stroking his shaft forward and back while Shae sucked on his head and swirled her tongue around the crown. Watching the whole scene inches away from her upturned face, Laura lifted her head a few more inches and engulfed Dylan's balls in her mouth, sucking them hard.

At this point, with virtually everybody in the room groaning and panting in pleasure from their combined connections with one person or another, Brad finally sunk his enormous pole all the way into my snatch, while his tight balls rubbed up against my dripping labia. Watching Shae bent over directly in front of me fucking Laura, I reached between her legs with my free hand and squeezed her balls as she began to pant more heavily. With the sweet smell of sex permeating the room, one person after another began to howl as they reached the height of their pleasure humping and sucking whatever hard or wet body part happened to be closest nearby.

By the time the six of us on the game board fell exhausted and spent onto the slippery plastic mat, I noticed that even *Maddy* had removed her clothes, impaled on her previous boyfriend's hard cock while her current beau straddled his face, pulling his head onto his own spurting cock as emptied his seed into his mouth.

Wow, I thought shaking my head in amazement. *This game really does have a way of creating some unexpected twists and turns.*

R*eady for more erotic chills and thrills? Pre-order the next spicy story in Jade's Erotic Adventures:*

This virtual assistant knows how to satisfy all your
needs...

ALSO BY VICTORIA RUSH

Wet your whistle a hundred different ways with Jade's Erotic Adventures. Browse the full collection of Victoria Rush steamy stories here:

Click to scan your favorites...

FOLLOW VICTORIA RUSH:

Want to keep informed of my latest erotic book releases? Sign up for my newsletter and receive a FREE bonus book:

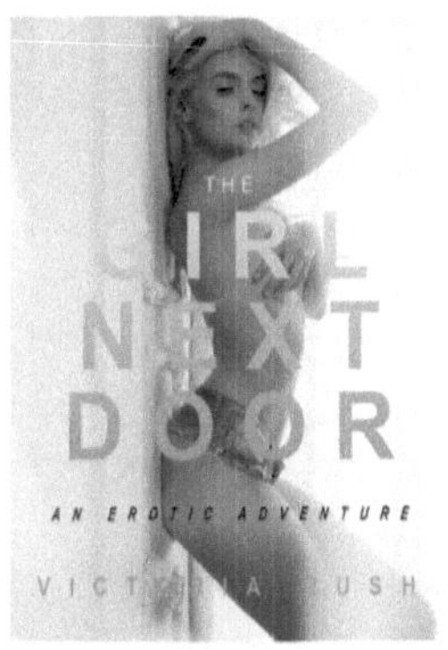

Spying on the neighbors just got a lot more interesting...